Raccoon
Moon

With special thanks to friends and raccoon lovers for your help with the book:
Lynda Graham-Barber, Bonnie Kruch, E. Jean Lanyon, Karen Murphy and Hilary Taylor.

for
Erika, Kurt and Laura

In memory of my husband, Larry Field

Raccoon Moon

Summary: Describes a year in the life of a raccoon family as the mother
teaches her cubs to climb trees, find food and survive predators.

Library of Congress Catalog Card Number 2002090173
ISBN 0-9662761-2-4 Cloth
ISBN 0-9662761-3-2 Paper

Published in the United States by Birdsong Books
Printed in China

Raccoon Moon

Nancy Carol Willis

Birdsong Books
Middletown, Delaware

Around April moon rises over an old silver maple tree. Inside the hollow trunk, raccoon cubs are being born. Rusty, Rudy and Spice are only four inches long. They cannot see or hear. Each weighs two ounces, about as much as a candy bar.

"Err, err, err," they cry. Mother raccoon gently nudges the cubs onto her belly, where they nurse on warm milk.

Three weeks later, the cubs open their eyes. As their fur grows, black markings begin to appear on their faces and tails. Rudy has seven tail rings. Spice has gray body fur. Rusty is reddish-brown.

Mother raccoon leaves the den to hunt for grasshoppers, bird eggs and earthworms. While she is gone, the cubs cuddle together to keep warm.

One month passes, and the moon is full again. The cubs have grown to weigh two pounds, sixteen times more than when they were born.

Rudy climbs up mother raccoon's back. Spice nips her thick fur with new baby teeth. For once, Rusty sits still while mother raccoon licks his face to clean it. "Churr, churr," he purrs.

The cubs peer from
the den opening as
mother raccoon climbs headfirst
down the tree to hunt for food.

Spice sniffs the salt marsh air, then
digs her sharp claws into the tree bark
and climbs out of the den. She wraps
her forearms around the trunk and inches
upward - higher, higher. Suddenly, her
hind feet slip. Spice dangles two stories high.

"Waaa," she shrieks. "Mother, help!" Mother
raccoon scrambles up the tree. She gently closes
her mouth around Spice's neck and carries the cub
back to the den. Soon the cubs will climb like experts.

It's the June summer solstice, the shortest night of the year. Mother raccoon calls for her cubs to follow. Raccoons are nocturnal, which means they hunt at night. If they are to one day survive on their own, the cubs must learn to forage for food. They follow mother raccoon down grassy paths lit by a yellow moon.

Along the way, Rusty follows a blinking firefly. Rudy sniffs a musky-smelling groundhog burrow. Overhead, a great-horned owl calls, "Whoo, whoo."

"Snort," warns mother raccoon. It's her way of telling the cubs, "Stay close." She knows owls and foxes may attack cubs that stray.

At the edge of a stream, Rudy spots a shiny green animal with round yellow eyes. He crouches. He pounces. Splash! The slippery frog gets away. Raccoons like to eat frogs, turtles, mussels and crayfish.

Nearby, mulberry branches droop to the mossy ground. Spice nibbles a hard white berry. Her lips curl from the bitter taste. She sees mother raccoon gobble the plump, purple berries and decides those must be the sweet, ripe ones. When they've eaten their fill, the family forges the stream.

The cubs waddle across a hollow log. It's slippery, and Rusty slides into the stream. Suddenly the log wobbles, and the other cubs tumble in too. Rusty paddles with his head up and tail straight out. He could travel about three miles in one hour if he needed to escape enemies or find food. Onshore, Spice shakes the water off by twisting from head to tail.

14

Spice spots a round, smooth snail. She swishes and dunks it in the shallow water. Spice isn't washing the food, just exploring it with her sensitive fingers.

Rudy snatches a fiddler crab from its muddy burrow. But the crab clamps its claw around Rudy's paw. "Grr-OWL," he howls!

Mother raccoon pins the crab to the
ground and chomps off the claws.
Now it's safe to eat the tasty meat.

With his belly full, Rusty wants to play. He lies in wait, then jumps on Spice. They roll and tumble, nip and growl. Rudy grabs his brother's tail, and they chase each other, squealing.

18

What looks like a fight is really a game. By snarling and snapping, the cubs learn how to defend themselves from predators.

Hearing the scuffle, a dog bolts through the brush. Mother raccoon chases her cubs up the nearest tree, where they'll be safe. Rusty, Rudy and Spice have never seen such a large animal.

Arching her back, mother raccoon stands tall and fierce. The hairs stiffen on the back of her neck.

"Growl," snarls the dog, baring his teeth.

"Hiss," spits mother raccoon. She lunges, snapping at the dog's throat. Finally, the dog backs off.

When it's safe, Mother raccoon hurries the family back to the den.

A crescent moon shimmers in the hazy August sunset. Now four months old, the cubs are weaned and no longer depend on their mother's milk.

22

Rudy and Spice rip the ears
of corn from the stalks.
Rusty tears away the husk
and devours the plump,
yellow kernels. He can eat
five pounds of food a night.
If they are to survive the winter,
the cubs must double their body
weight before cold sets in.

The raccoon family visits a farmyard, where Spice has learned to push open the gate latch. Sniff, sniff -What's that delightfully stinky smell? It's the garbage can! Rudy tips over the can, and a feast tumbles out - a banana peel, eggshells, and an apple core. Mother raccoon snatches a peanut butter jar, turning her back to protect the prize.

The bird feeder may be squirrel-proof, but it's no problem for Rusty. He sits on the squirrel baffle and scoops sunflower seeds from the feeding tray.

25

A cool September breeze wakes the cubs from their day beds on tree limbs. It's time for them to find warm dens for the winter. Spice returns with her mother to the old silver maple tree. Rusty and Rudy search for a new den together.

They explore a hayloft, but it's too drafty. They try a chimney, a shed, an abandoned car and an old fox burrow.

Finally, they settle upon an oak tree covered in honeysuckle vines.

As the temperature falls to freezing, Rusty, Rudy, Spice and mother raccoon curl up cozy in their dens. They may sleep for weeks at a time, even though they do not hibernate. When they get cold, tossing and turning warms them up.

During brief warm spells, the raccoons will scrounge for dried corn, acorns, seeds or mice. For now, they wrap their tails around them like blankets and dream of the warm spring raccoon moon.

More Fun Facts about Raccoons

A Year in the Life of the Raccoon

Jan	Feb	Mar	Apr	May	Jun	Jul	Aug	Sep	Oct	Nov	Dec

Mating

Gestation: average 63 days

Birth: average litter 3 to 5 cubs

Growth of cubs in the den:
2 weeks - markings appear
3 weeks - eyes open
4 weeks - teeth appear
8 weeks - walk & climb

10 weeks - cubs follow mother to forage
16 weeks - cubs completely weaned

Raccoons fatten up
Fur grows thicker

In Den

How Did the Raccoon Get It's Name?

The Algonquin Indians of Virginia called raccoons *arakunem,* or "he scratches with the hands." Early colonists couldn't pronounce the word and called the animal "raccoon." The raccoon's scientific name is *Procyon lotor,* meaning "before dog, a washer." Actually, raccoons and bears may be descended from an early race of dogs that evolved about 30 million years ago. The raccoon doesn't wash its food. It dabbles in shallow water, feeling for it; then manipulates the food with sensitive paws.

Where do Raccoons Live?

A raccoon has a *home range,* or territory of about one square mile. In it is everything the raccoon needs to survive: a den site, feeding grounds and drinking water. All of the raccoons live in a range that extends from southern Canada and the United States, throughout Mexico and Panama.

Raccoon Relatives

Ringtail
Range: Southern Oregon southeast to Louisiana, south to central Mexico
Dens: In trees, caves and brush piles
Food: Insects, rodents, crustaceans, fruits of juniper, oak and prickly pear

Coati
Range: Southern Arizona and New Mexico south to Panama
Dens: In trees, caves and ledges
Food: Insects, spiders, and prickly pear

Crab-eating raccoon
Range: Central and South America
Dens: In trees near streams and swamps
Food: Crabs, mollusks, insects and fruit

How to Help Baby Raccoons

Let the Mother Do Her Job

If you see young raccoons without an adult, watch for several hours to see if the mother returns. Cubs may wander from the den if their mother is gone too long. A mother raccoon will not abandon her cubs unless she is killed or the den site is disturbed.

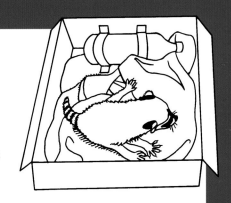

Young Raccoons Need Professional Care

You'll need to take orphaned or injured cubs to a licensed wildlife rehabilitator *as soon as possible.* Rehabilitators are trained to care for wild animals.

• Children should never approach or touch a wild animal. Instead, call an adult for help.

• Baby raccoons will usually not bite, but any wild mammal can transmit rabies to humans and pets. For this reason, always wear protective gloves when handling wild animals. Place the cubs in a cloth-lined pet carrier or covered box with air holes.

• Cubs need to remain warm. Fill a plastic juice bottle with hot tap water. Tape the bottle to the sides of the box to keep it from rolling onto the cubs.

Emergency Feeding

If you can't take the cubs to a licensed rehabilitator immediately, feed them one of the *temporary* diets listed below. Make sure the cubs are warm; they can't digest food when cold. Wearing gloves, feed the cub by holding it upright or on its stomach. Formula should be warm, but not hot. Use a pet nursing bottle or a human baby bottle with a nipple used to feed premature babies. Raccoons will over-eat; feed until the belly feels full, but not tight. When finished, wash your hands with antibacterial soap.

If the cubs' eyes have not opened, feed:

• Any commercial kitten or puppy milk replacement formula found in pet stores or veterinary clinics.

• Feed 10 cc's (about 1/2 ounce) *every two hours from 6 a.m. to 11 p.m.*

• After every feeding, young cubs need help to urinate and defecate. Gently rub the abdomen with a soft cloth to stimulate elimination.

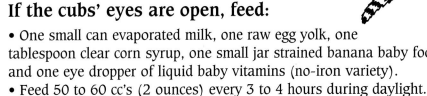

If the cubs' eyes are open, feed:

• One small can evaporated milk, one raw egg yolk, one tablespoon clear corn syrup, one small jar strained banana baby food, and one eye dropper of liquid baby vitamins (no-iron variety).

• Feed 50 to 60 cc's (2 ounces) every 3 to 4 hours during daylight.

Why Can't I Keep a Baby Raccoon as a Pet?

Your cuddly baby raccoon will grow into an aggressive adult. If it hasn't learned the skills to survive in the wild, it can't be released. There are 13 diseases people and pets can catch from raccoons, such as distemper and rabies. If a wild mammal bites you, contact your local animal control service so they can capture the animal. See your doctor immediately.

Whom to Contact for Help

To find a wildlife rehabilitation facility near you, contact your local zoo, veterinarian, the U.S. Department of Fish and Wildlife, or the National Wildlife Rehabilitators Association (NWRA).

Glossary

Raccoon Trivia

Height: 9 - 12 inches at the shoulders

Length: 30 - 33 inches nose to tail; tail 10 inches

Weight: 12 - 16 pounds, smaller in Florida

Largest: 62 pounds, 6 ounces; 55 inches from nose to tail; November 1950 in Wisconsin

Age: 10 - 12 years; average 4 years; 14 oldest

Fur color: Gray, reddish-brown, black or yellow

Facemask: The black color may absorb light, aiding in night vision; each marking is unique

Tail: 5 - 7 black rings with black tip

IQ: Curiosity and dexterity rank it above a cat, but below a monkey

Paws: Forepaws are 4 times more sensitive than human hands; raccoons are plantigrade animals that walk the on entire foot as a man

Litter size: 2 - 7; 3 - 5 cubs is average

Foods: Raccoons eat almost anything: crayfish, crabs, frogs, clams, turtles, milk corn, acorns, field grains, berries, bird eggs, grapes, apples, plums, persimmons, grubs, crickets, slugs, earthworms, mice, salamanders, moss, garbage